The Day
Eddie met
the Author

Eddie Lewis   Grade 3

How do you write

books that have parts

meant for me?

Also by Louise Borden

The Little Ships
The Heroic Rescue at Dunkirk in World War II
illustrated by Michael Foreman

Good-bye, Charles Lindbergh
illustrated by Thomas B. Allen

Good Luck, Mrs. K!
illustrated by Adam Gustavson

Sleds on Boston Common
A Story from the American Revolution
illustrated by Robert Andrew Parker

Fly High!
The Story of Bessie Coleman
co-authored by Mary Kay Kroeger
illustrated by Teresa Flavin

The Day Eddie met the Author

by Louise Borden

illustrated by
Adam Gustavson

Margaret K. McElderry Books
New York London Toronto Sydney Singapore

Margaret K. McElderry Books
An imprint of Simon & Schuster Children's Publishing Division
1230 Avenue of the Americas
New York, New York 10020

Book design by Sonia Chaghatzbanian and Jim Hoover.
The text of this book was set in Horley Old Style.
The illustrations were rendered in watercolor.

Printed in Hong Kong

10 9 8 7 6 5 4 3 2 1

Library of Congress Cataloging-in-Publication Data

Borden, Louise.
The day Eddie met the author / by Louise Borden ; illustrated by Adam Gustavson.
p. cm.
Summary: Eddie is very excited when a real author comes to his school because he has a very important question to ask her.
ISBN 0-689-83405-5
[1. Books and reading—Fiction. 2. Authorship—Fiction. 3. Schools—Fiction.]
I. Gustavson, Adam, ill.
II. Title.
PZ7.B64827 Day 2001
[E]—dc21
99-046922

*In memory of Linda Dodd
and for all the wonderful students and teachers along the way*

–L. B.

Author's note:

Listed on the endpapers of this book are the names of some of the schools that I have visited. I remember and thank all those other schools that are not included on this list.

Tuesday, October 10th

Tuesday, October 10th
was going to be a great day for Eddie and his class.
It was the day a real author was coming to
Riverside Elementary School.
Eddie had been waiting, waiting, waiting. . . .
The whole school had been waiting.
Especially Eddie's teacher, Mrs. Morrow.
She *loved* real authors.
She loved how real authors made the words flow,
and how the words sounded just right,
and went with pictures in their own way.

Mrs. Morrow said she couldn't live without books
and the wonderful stories in them.
She said third graders had their own stories to tell:
"We are all authors with important stories inside us."
Eddie chewed on his pencil and thought hard.
How could *his* stories ever be like a real author's?

Eddie had been reading, reading, reading. . . .

His whole class had been reading.

Ten different books by the author who was coming to visit.

In every one of those books,

Eddie found a part that seemed just for him.

Everyone in the class found their own parts in the books, too.

"How does the author do that?" Eddie asked Mrs. Morrow
one morning as the bell rang for recess.

"That's a great question, Eddie," his teacher said.

"You'll have to ask her when she comes."

Eddie wrote down his author question on a bright yellow
piece of paper and put it in his desk,
right on top of his "Ideas to Write About" notebook.

"That's a question you won't want to lose," Mrs. Morrow told
him with her best smile.

Eddie Lewis   Grade 3

How do you write

books that have parts

meant for me?

For two weeks,
everyone from kindergarten to fifth grade
had been getting ready for the author's visit.
The second graders made book jackets.
The fourth graders made poems and posters.
Mrs. Morrow's class hung a mural in the cafeteria
that showed characters from the author's stories.
Everyone said, "This isn't work, this is FUN!"
Even Ms. Kindel, the school secretary.
And Arthur, the custodian.
And Mr. Chickerella, the brand new principal.

Eddie was proud of his school.
He hoped the author would say:
"Wow, what a visit!
Riverside Elementary is my Number 1 favorite!"

On Monday, October 9th,

Mrs. Morrow's students were full of questions:

"What does the author look like?" everyone asked.

"Is she short?"

"Is she tall?"

"Is she old?"

"Is she young?"

"Is she skinny?"

"Is she plump?"

"Is she nice?"

"Maybe," said Mrs. Morrow to all their questions.

"We'll find out tomorrow."

At last! The big day!

Mrs. Morrow wrote *Tuesday, October 10th* on the chalkboard in her best cursive.

All morning,
Eddie waited for his class to go to the assembly in the gym.
He watched the minutes on the wall clock tick-ticking by.
He folded and unfolded his yellow paper.
He checked the words he wanted to ask three times.
It was an important question.
Eddie chewed on his pencil.
What if the author didn't call on him
when he raised his hand?

Finally Ms. Kindel's polite voice came over the school intercom:
"Grades two and three are to go to the gym now. . . ."
Eddie folded up his question and put it in his pocket
on the way to the author assembly.

Mrs. Morrow led her class into the gym.

There was the real author!

She was testing Mr. Chickerella's microphone
and getting ready for the assembly.

Arthur was setting up chairs for the teachers.

Eddie checked out the author from head to foot.

He thought real authors would look different from
everybody else.

This author just looked like a teacher or a mom.

Eddie sat between two of his classmates
and he sat up straight.

The author was wearing a vest that was a patchwork
of pictures from some of her books.

Eddie looked to find his favorite one—there it was!

There were whispers in the audience.

Then Mr. Chickerella welcomed their special guest.

No one in Mrs. Morrow's class talked or squirmed,
not even Tyler Mason.

Everyone was ready to listen,
and the author began:

"I can tell you've all had your noses in my books. . . .
I've been reading your wonderful writing
in the school hallways,
and seen your terrific illustrations. . . ."

Eddie sat up straighter, he was so proud of Riverside Elementary.

"Some of you may be wondering how to become a writer.
The best way to become a writer is to be a reader. . . ."
Eddie was a reader. . . . The author was talking about him!

The minutes of the assembly zoomed by.

Eddie never wanted it to end.

Today he felt like a real writer.

Finally it was time for questions and answers.

Eddie put his hand up, fast as lightning,

but there were other hands in front of him and behind him,

and on both sides.

Everyone wanted the author to call on them.

Eddie waved his yellow paper in the air.

His question was important.

Mrs. Morrow had said it was not a question to lose.

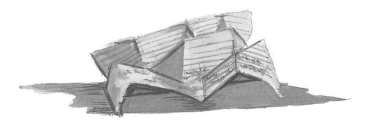

"Which book is your
favorite book?"

"Do you ever run out
of ideas?"

"Which book was the
hardest to write?"

"How old are your
kids?"

No one asked the question that Eddie wanted answered.

But the assembly was over,

and Eddie hadn't been called on.

Mr. Chickerella began to dismiss the second

and third graders.

Eddie's question!

His important question on the most exciting day

of the school year!

He wanted to know the answer.

Eddie read the words he had written on his yellow paper.

Slowly Eddie folded up his question and put it back
in his pocket.

Suddenly he felt a grown-up's hand on his shoulder.

But it wasn't Mrs. Morrow.

Or Mr. Chickerella.

It was the author!

She was standing right next to Eddie in the third-grade line,
asking him his name.

Then she said:

"I saw your hand up in the assembly,
waving a yellow paper.
I knew you had an important question to ask . . .
but we ran out of time. . . ."

The third graders began to crowd around Eddie
and the author.
Mrs. Morrow shushed everyone
as the author unfolded the yellow paper
and read Eddie's words out loud.

"Now *that* is a thinking question, Eddie!" the author said.
Her smile was like a big, warm hug.
Eddie felt as tall as a grown-up
standing in his third-grade line.

Everyone was quiet while the author put her hand
on her chin
and thought about Eddie's question.
Maybe everyone was thinking about the parts
of the author's books
that seemed like they were meant just for them.
That's what Eddie was thinking about.

Then the author said:
"Eddie, if you write about parts of yourself,
I bet your reader will have some of those parts, too.
I guess that's a small answer to the big question you asked.
And by the way, I've always loved the name Eddie. . . .
Someday I may use it when I'm writing a book. . . ."

Eddie looked at Mrs. Morrow and gave her a wide smile.
Now maybe *his* stories could be like the author's.
And he would try to write from his heart.

On the afternoon of Tuesday, October 10,
Eddie began a rough draft of a new story
during Mrs. Morrow's writing workshop.
He didn't know how it would end,
but he had plenty to write about
from what had happened that day.
He already knew a title to use.
He'd written it in his notebook
as soon as he got back to the classroom:

adford • Ann Weigel • Bevis • Colerain • St. James • St. Thomas More • Strub
irview • Sacred Heart • Lincoln • Reynolds • Herig • Handley • Nelle Haley •
erbringer • Heavenrich • Houghton • Kempton • Loomis • John Moore • Stone • Z
ab • Lynchburg • Vermont • Elm • Hilltop • Immaculate Heart of Mary • Olney
ville • New Haven • Buckeye Valley West • Wilson • Caywood • Rosedale • Hoove
pewell • Montgomery • Liberty • Our Lady of the Rosary • Symmes • Maple Dale
od • Milford South • Fairview • Clovernook • Ross School • Lloyd Mann • Ayer
ls • St. Margaret of York • Poasttown • Batavia • Peebles • Ruth Moyer • Wi
irfield North • Clinton-Massie • George Washington • Oakland • Fair Park •
itewater Valley • St. Vivian • Custer Park • Kentland • Elkhart Young Authors
unty Young Authors • Cincinnati Hills • Spring Mill • Martinsville • Holmes
ors • Westwood • Central • Louisa Wright • Spencer Schools • Dunlavy • Roosev
od • Mississinawa • Franklin Monroe • Mason Heights • Gettysburg • North Fra
wland Glen • Howland Springs • Ansonia • Bramble • Eastwood Padeia • Chevio
rfield • Lincoln • East Middle • Cortland • Boyd E. Smith • Cure of Ars • Se
dd • Ascension • Carlisle • Wynford • Versailles • Holmes County • St. Mary'
irbrook • Parkwood • Elkhart Young Authors • Adena • Timonium • Union • India
n • Darke County • Goodridge • Montgomery • Flemingsburg • Ward • Hilltop •
osevelt • Pleasant Ridge • Pickerington • Deer Run • Indian Run • St. Andre
rtland • Hiawatha • Central Wardcliff • Hamilton Central • Southgate • Hamil
ckliffe • St. Bernard • Elmwood Place • Summerside • Huron County Young Autho
gton • Tri-County North • Whiteford • North Dearborn • Bright • Independence
henck • St. Brendan's • Blessed Sacrament • Twin Valley South • Withamsville
addock • Wyandot Run • Alum Creek • Scioto Ridge • Arrowhead • North Side •
bert Johnson • North Dearborn • Kyle • Piqua Catholic • Longfellow • St. Al
ller • Centerville K. V. • Boyd E. Smith • Terrace Park • Sarasota Readers •
reet • Pleasant Valley • Batesville • St. Gabriel • Seneca-Huron • Attica •
ue • Hanalei • Lincoln • Court Street • St. Clare • Elda • Blanchester • Whit
Ayer • Burlington • Withamsville-Tobasco • Stuart • Pleasant Hill • Miami •
llowville • Mercer • Mountain Shadow • Springer • McGuffey • Dumont • Visali
reet • Pearl Street • Olney Avenue • John Shank • Glenwood • Indian Mound • W
nd Young Authors • St Teresa • Sacred Heart • Lincoln • Reynolds • Herig • Ha
illie • Coulter • Fuerbringer • Heavenrich • Houghton • Kempton • Loomis •
shington County • Mt. Orab • Lynchburg • Vermont • Elm • Hilltop • Immaculate
thel-Tate • Fayetteville • New Haven • Ansonia • Bramble • Eastwood Paideia
ddle • Garfield • Lincoln • East Middle • Cortland • Boyd E. Smith • Cure of
C.E. Budd • Ascension • Carlisle • Wynford • Versailles • Holmes County • St